SISSY HUSBAND

2

A wife always knows what her husband needs

Lady Alexa

Also by Lady Alexa

Becoming Joanne
Becoming Joanne 1
Becoming Joanne 2
Becoming Joanne 3

Femboy Love
Femboy Love 1

Feminized and Pretty
Feminized and Pretty 1
Feminized and Pretty 3
Feminized and Pretty 4

Forced Feminization
Forced Feminization Bundle 1

Lockdown Feminization

Lockdown Feminization 3
Lockdown Feminization 1

Sissy femboy transgender husband
Sissy Husband 2
Sissy Husband 3
SIssy Husband 1
Sissy Husband 4

Sissy Princess
Sissy Princess 2
Sissy Princess 1

Stepmother's Sissy
Stepmother's Sissy
Stepmother's Sissy 2
Stepmother's Sissy 3

Standalone
A Very Dominant Woman
Sissy Pink

Watch for more at https://www.ladyalexauk.com.

If you enjoy transgender erotica, you can also subscribe to my blog charting my real-life Female Led relationship and feminisation lifestyle with my feminised husband Alice here: www.ladyalexauk.com[1]

You can also subscribe to my newsletter and receive exclusive forced feminisation stories, news and offers by subscribing from my blog
www.ladyalexauk.com

CONTENTS

Sissy Husband 2 is the second book of an updated re-telling of an earlier series called A Sissy Cuckold Husband. The original was a classic forced feminisation story where a husband is feminised by a Mistress and his wife as a double act. They turn him into a submissive and cuckolded sissy.

I revisit my older books from time to time to update the covers and some of the inner text. While updating my A Sissy Cuckold Husband series, I noticed there was an alternative storyline within the plot – that of husband who visits professional mistresses to live out his sissy fantasy but keeps his femboy dreams a secret from his wife Gemma.

Once Gemma finds out her husband's desires to be a femboy sissy through his former girlfriend, Gemma and her new friend set about realising his and their dream. Her husband Paul pushes back as he tackles his inner societal programming that being a sissy femboy is shameful despite his internal feelings.

The stories now have more of a transgender awakening theme and of a mutually agreed relationship that satisfies everyone but is very different to what society considers the norm.

1 – The Beginning of the End

Today was the day Paul Paige would be reborn as Pansy, the sissy princess. He was to be like a pretty butterfly emerging from a chrysalis.

Pansy was deeply in love with his stunning wife Gemma and would do anything for her. Dominatrix Karlene Adair, would be the power behind Gemma's loving transformation of Paul. Ever since they had met and become friends just a few days ago, Karlene had guided Gemma towards her destiny as a strong and dominant wife. As Paul longed for. He didn't know that yet, of course.

Karlene's long chestnut-brown flowed and waved over her shoulders and down to the small of her back. Her low-cut golden crop top sparkled in the light from the window. A diamond stud glinted from her exposed belly button like a single small unblinking eye. Her smooth skin shimmered like milky chocolate. A matching golden skirt hung from slender hips. It shimmied as her slim smooth legs poked through between the fine vertical strips of metallic-like material.

She paced the floor by the windows, drawing power from the vibrance of the city beneath her feet. Karlene had an ally in her quest, in her reason for living. She had found Gemma to be a willing wife who wanted her husband to live his dream. His secret dream to be a sissy femboy. But now Gemma knew his secret.

Karlene would see her passion for transforming powerful men into obedient pansies put into action through her new pupil: Gemma the Goddess. Pansy Paul was the perfect target: wealthy, good-looking, confident and powerful. Soon he was to become a weak, submissive sissy. His fantasy. He was paying anonymous professional mistresses to feminise him so he could live his fantasy for a couple of hours. Soon it would be his lifestyle.

Karlene felt damp with excitement, it was what turned her on.

Gemma was uncommonly in love with her husband and she'd taught Gemma of the need to turn him into a sissy princess. It was an act of love. Nevertheless, Karlene would keep an eye on her; to keep Gemma on the straight and narrow path. The path to making and keeping her husband as a sissy. That's where Frank came in. A 6ft 4in porn star and yoga instructor, rippling muscle and eleven-inch cock. She hadn't explained that Frank was a porn star, Gemma wasn't yet ready for that bit of news. Gemma was very proper which was endearing.

After suffering Pansy's little dick for years, Gemma was frustrated and lusting after long thick hard meat. And now she'd seen it in the flesh when Karlene showed Frank to her, there was no going back for Gemma.

Karlene checked her watch, nearly 5 pm, it was time to leave. Her Mistress lessons to Gemma were over, it was time to put her training into action. She slipped her overcoat over her skimpy clothes and left her apartment. She closed her front door with a gentle click.

Sweet Pansy Paul. If he only knew what was about to hit him this evening. He's going to love it. Eventually.

2 — Surprise

THE SOUND OF RUBBER crunching on gravel announced Paul's evening arrival from the office. He pulled the large black German saloon up outside the front window with a sliding scrunch.

Karlene sat next to Gemma on a wide four-seater sofa in the living room of Paul and Gemma Paige's home in the city's exclusive suburb. Autumn was sliding into winter and a motion detector light came on in the gloom outside and glinted in through the half-drawn curtains. The drizzle outside seemed to hang in the air like mist in the light.

Inside, the living room was bathed in a cosy low light from a silver-coloured uplighter in the corner. The furniture was large and dark, a thick cream carpet covered the floor. Warmth flowed from three large white radiators. Karlene had her hands on her bare thighs. Her skirt hung loose and short, her top was low-cut and her breasts spilled out. She knew she looked stunning and sexual. That was the point,

Gemma grinned at her and Karlene detected a trace of nerves and excitement in her friend's eyes. It's not every evening you turn your husband into a sissy princess. The engine outside died and a car door slammed. After several seconds, the metallic scratch of a metal key in the front latch echoed through the silent house.

Karlene took Gemma's hand, it felt warm and sticky. Gemma was nervous, it was understandable.

Gemma wore a tight red dress, thin straps held it up around her broad shoulders. Her 36DD breasts also spilled from a low-cut top. Paul loved big tits and Karlene intended to have hers and Gemma's displayed for their purposes. Men were so obvious and Paul was no different.

Gemma's dress outlined her lean shaped thighs. Her earrings and necklace glinted heavy with 24-carat gold. If she hadn't been so elegant, she might have passed for a high-class hooker that evening. That had also been the point. Men like obvious.

Gemma had been to the hairdresser's in the afternoon to have her thick blond hair styled. Her straightened hair rested on top of bare shoulders with the ends flicked up. She wore black shoes with four-inch thin heels like two ice picks. This was the new-look Gemma. Sensual, hot and unavailable to her husband.

"The teaching is over, Gemma darling. It's your time to be the sexy, heartbreaking, hot-wife Goddess I taught you to be."

Karlene felt the need to kiss Gemma and leaned in with a soft gentle peck on her red lips. The two women looked into each other's eyes, a memory of those shared moments last week. They would come again.

Gemma sat up straight, an inner strength flowing through her. Karlene's eyes fell over Gemma. She was stunning tonight and Karlene's stomach turned over with desire. She shook her head clear. "It's time to enact our plan, Gemma darling. Exactly as I outlined. By the end of the evening, Pansy will be your sweet sissy princess husband and in the palm of your hand where you want him. And where he wants to be." She leant across and planted another soft kiss on Gemma's lips. They lingered a while, the tips of their tongues gently licked against each other through their partly open lips.

They moved apart, eyes locked. "I'm ready." Gemma's voice was clear and strong.

At that moment, Paul's voice carried through from the hallway. "Gemma honey? Gemma? I'm home."

"In here, Paulie, dearest."

The door swung open and Paul marched in, short, slim and confident. He carried himself upright, as if trying to find that extra inch of height. His long wavy brown hair was brushed back and swirled over his tailored dark-blue suit below his collar. His vague centre parting and length were dated, but worked and gave him a certain soft style. More pretty boy than feminine. White double shirt cuffs protruded a precise one inch from each sleeve. Heavy square gold cufflinks glinted under the glow of the ceiling lamp.

Paul stopped dead, the smile fading from his face like melting butter over a stove. His eyes swung from Gemma to Karlene and back, his face creased in surprise.

"Karlene?" He looked at each one again. "What are you doing here? I didn't know you were visiting tonight."

Gemma slid along the wide sofa away from Karlene without replying. She patted the empty space she had vacated to sit between them. She grinned a sweet symmetric smile, her perfect white teeth gleamed bright white.

Paul hesitated for a short moment, his eyes rested on his wife's chalk-white panties visible beneath her short tight hem. Her dress had ridden up. Karlene could see he was confused by his wife's change of clothing style. Supermodel in the morning to high-class hooker by evening.

He walked towards the two ladies, his eyes fixed on Gemma's crotch, his approach slow and careful. Gemma patted the sofa again and looked up and batted her eyelids. Karlene stroked her fingers through the length of her chestnut mane of rich brown hair.

Paul's eyebrows creased tight as he pondered the scenario, but the sight of the two sensational women drew him in. He didn't suspect anything untoward just strange. He sat down. The two ladies slid into him, close, their legs against his. Gemma's hand fell onto his lap and slid up to his crotch. His eyes swivelled to Karlene then back to Gemma. He tried to speak but Gemma leaned across and her lips locked onto his.

She pulled away. "Relax, Paulie. This is going to be the night that changes your life."

Karlene's eyes widened. "Forever."

3— Pansy Paul

Karlene ran her fingernails down Paul's arm as Gemma's tongue pressed deep into his mouth. Her hand pressed over his penis and kneaded into it. Paul's eyes flicked around the room, wild and wide.

Gemma broke from his lips and put her mouth to his ear and ran them down to his neck and kissed it. Her hand pushed harder into his crotch. He was startled. He didn't know what to do. Perhaps they wanted a threesome, he wondered.

"You're pleased to see me, Paulie," said Gemma looking at his penis. "How sweet, little twinkie is hard."

He tried to complain about saying that in front of Karlene but she placed one arm around his neck and hugged him closer stifling his words for a moment.

He broke free. "Gemma, what are you doing? Karlene's here. What is this? Why exactly is Karlene here?" Paul was breathless, but he didn't push Gemma's hand away from his trouser front. She moved her hand over his flies onto his hard little dick. She slipped his flies down with a smooth movement and slipped her hand inside.

"Gemma, what the hell are you up to? You can't do that in front of Karlene."

"Oh don't worry about Karlene, Paulie, she doesn't mind. It's not as if she hasn't seen your little twinkie. You dated a few years ago or have you forgotten? We thought we'd surprise you this evening, my love. Think of it as a special treat." Gemma looked up at Karlene, a single eyebrow raised in conspiracy. "Paulie, I'm going to do this to you out of my love for you," Gemma whispered in his ear.

As he tried to speak, Karlene's hand fell from his arm and onto his thigh. He jumped. She squeezed his thigh through his trousers and inched toward the open fly. "Yes, relax Paulie, sit back and let us look after you." Karlene's lips brushed close to his and away again.

His eyes lit in excitement and apprehension

"You're warm, my love, let me take your jacket off." Gemma pulled him forward and slipped off his jacket. She dropped behind the sofa. Karlene's hand replaced Gemma's inside his fly. She located his little erection. She touched it with her little finger through his underpants. He jumped and gasped.

"What do we have here, little Paulie?" Karlene said "I remember this little fellow."

He let out a small groan of pleasure. This was a dream come true for him. His wife and Karlene making it a threesome. What a fantastic surprise. Karlene flicked the button open at the top of his trousers, letting them spill open. His little erection pointed out.

Karlene's eyes fell on it. She turned back to Gemma. "He has such a tiny little twinkie. I'd forgotten how small it was. What is it, two inches soft, four erect? I remember when it was soft, I couldn't see it properly." She giggled. "It's why I took lovers."

Paul tried to sit up, a pang of annoyance at Karlene's slight but a look of something else in his eyes. Excitement. Gemma guided him back with a single hand on his chest and whispered, "*Schhhhhh*, my love. Relax. Enjoy."

His eyes stared out and swivelled around, uncomprehending at what was happening to him. He sat back against the sofa, giving in to the unexpected delight if two sexy women undressing him. Loving and hating what was happening at the same time. Gemma put both her hands on his tie, undid it and pouted as she she pulled on one end and it slipped through his collar and out. She dropped it behind her onto his jacket.

Karlene put a thumb and forefinger on the end of his erection. She pulled back his foreskin and rubbed it up and down in a slow gentle motion. Up and down, light and delicate. His tense expression faded, his eyes fluttered in delight.

Gemma pushed her fingers between his shirt buttons and flicked them open one by one. She undid half of the buttons and then kissed his chest. She ran her fingers through the few hairs there. A small noise of utter pleasure emanated from somewhere deep in his throat. She pushed her fingers along his chest muscles.

Gemma undid the remainder of the buttons. She pulled the shirt from the sleeves and dropped it on top of his tie and jacket behind her. He was bare chested. He closed his eyes. Karlene knew they had him, he was in their control. Karlene got up from the sofa and knelt at his feet. She blew on his little erection. She undid his shoelaces and pulled off each shoe followed by his socks. She took his trouser legs and tugged on them.

"No, you can't be serious." Paul sat up again. "This is wonderful, but Gemma, it isn't right."

Gemma ran a hand over his chest and kissed his lips. "Too much chest hair." She pouted seductively. "Bottom up Paulie, let Karlene remove your trousers. We want to see your sexy legs and that cute little twinkie of yours."

He lifted his behind as if in a trance and Karlene pulled his trousers off. He sat back in only his black boxer shorts. They were open at the front, his little erection poking through.

Karlene and Gemma stopped what they were doing and stood up together. Karlene unzipped her skirt and let it drop to the floor. She lifted her top over her head and dropped that too. His eyes widened as if ready to pop. She stood in small black g-string panties and a matching bra. The bra had a small frill at the top and pushed up her large round breasts.

Paul's mouth pursed in wonder. Gemma turned her back to Karlene who unzipped her dress. Gemma wriggled out of the dress and kicked it away. She stood in a white g-string and a tight bra around her 36DD breasts. Paul's tongue lolled in his open mouth. He imagined sex with these two stunning ladies.

Karlene knelt back down and pushed Paul's legs open. "Too hairy, Paulie." He ignored her words and believed this was going to be a threesome. She slid between his legs and ran her hands over his calves and then up to his thighs. His little erection twitched.

"Such pretty legs." Karlene ran her finger over his calves, up over his thighs to the shape of his balls inside the boxer shorts.

Gemma sat next to him, her hand glided over his chest. She hummed. "Such a muscled chest my love. That needs to go. We don't want muscles, do we sweetie?" She cupped her hand over one small chest muscle and ran a finger around the outline. "You need something else here, my sweetie."

He hadn't grasped her meaning.

Karlene's hand went back up to his erection. She ran her forefinger over the exposed end. "Yes Gemma, he's so cute. Look at this little clitty. Cute but not smooth enough."

"What do you mean clitty?"

They ignored him. "Stand up pretty boy," Gemma purred.

He was in a state of ecstasy and ignored the pretty boy gibe. His sexy wife and sexy Karlene were seducing him. He stood up, not wanting this to stop. It was a dream. Karlene placed two fingers in the elastic waistband of his boxers. She fixed eyes with him. She edged the waistband down little by little. Paul gasped. She pulled the boxers down over his little erection. It sprung as she passed the waistband over it. He stepped out of them and stood naked.

Karlene moved him to face the sofa and the two ladies sat back down and faced his erect penis. Gemma ran a finger underneath it in a tickling motion. "It's so sweet." She looked up at him, innocence written on her face.

He coughed in complaint, not keen on Gemma referring to his manhood as sweet. Gemma took it between two fingers and rolled it like a cigarette.

"It's so girly." Karlene put her fingers to his balls and squeezed lightly. "Why do you have such girly parts, Pansy?" She inspected his balls. "These are little sissy balls."

Paul looked hurt. "There's no need to be nasty, ladies. And stop with the Pansy name. That was something from years ago. It's gone."

"Shhhh, sweet Pansy," whispered Gemma as she stroked his erection with two fingers then scratched her fingernails lightly over it as Karlene fondled his balls.

"I used to call his little dick *Miss Clitty* when we were in college. It's not a man's cock. I used to tell him *Miss Clitty* was small, pretty and cute. It's more like a girl's clitty. He liked that, Pansy with the cute miss clitty. It made him very hard. It got to three and a half inches hard. Or maybe four?" She waited in thought. "No, definitely only three and a half."

Paul's erection stiffened and twitched at her words.

"Oh look, she likes us calling her sissy and a girl." Gemma's lips were an inch from his erection. "I think it must be a girl's clitty." She put two fingers to his lips to stop him speaking.

Karlene squeezed his balls as if squashing a tennis ball before serving. Gemma ran her fingers up and down his erection. He groaned in the pleasure of their attention, but his eyes told a different story. He was worried about the turn the conversation had taken.

"Yes," Gemma said, warming to the theme. "Pansy is a femboy sissy. When we make love I'm always on top. She lays back like a little girl." She looked up at him, smiled and pulled gently on his erection. "And she cums too quickly. What fun is that for me? Making love with a sissy-girl with a tiny clitty." She pouted in fake annoyance.

Paul was becoming irritated despite also enjoying it. He said. "Stop calling me *she* and *her*."

They ignored him. Karlene's hands flowed over his testicles. "I see, Gemma, darling. He's been hiding in his sissy closet for too long. Only coming out for paid mistresses."

He tried to sit up and argue but Karlene pushed him back. Karlene stopped touching his balls. "But don't worry, Mistress Karlene is here to help Goddess Gemma improve the situation." She looked deeply into Paul's eyes. "Did naughty Pansy visit professional mistresses to get her sissy kick? I think so, Pansy boy"

"Look here," said Paul trying to sit up again.

Karlene stroked Paul's face with affection, then flicked his erection with a little swipe. "Who's been a naughty sissy?"

She put her hands to her bare hips and looked down at him. Her face in his, her huge dusky breasts below his chin. She lifted one hand from a hip and placed a single finger under his chin and raised it. "You're a sissy princess and..." She removed her finger and pointed between his eyes. She added sweetly in a low sexy voice. "Incapable of sexually satisfying your gorgeous goddess of a wife." She shook her head. "Bad Pansy."

Paul began to tremble, events were taking an unexpected turn for the worse. But, at the same time, he was enjoying it. His erection was firm and strong. His wife and Karlene were beautiful, sexy and clad in skimpy lingerie underwear. Gemma stood up next to Karlene. She giggled like a young girl and smiled with a look of love down at Paul. She put her head to one side and a hand to her hip. She ruffled her blond hair, her eyes wide and dancing with mischief.

Karlene bent down and ran a hand over his forehead and wiped his sweat. He put his hands down to cover his erection and his embarrassment. Gemma pulled them away with a sweet smile.

"We want to see little Miss Clitty because she's cute and girly." Gemma looked him up and down, her grin widening, her eyes sparkling. "You're a femboy sissy, Paulie." She giggled softly. "We're going to call you Pansy, as Karlene did at college."

"What the hell is going on?" Paul said anger mixing with intense desire.

Karlene walked round behind him. "Yes. Pansy. It's a good name for a sissy princess." Karlene moved like a ballet dancer, her long bare legs pacing around him. Karlene spotted Paul's eyes move down to her bottom. The g-string disappeared between her taut cheeks, as if she were naked apart from the thin string at the top of her hips. The front part of her panties was a sliver of satin material. It barely hid her jewels from his view. She didn't plan to show him, it was enough to know what he was missing and would never get.

Paul shuffled, his discomfort showing. "Please Gemma." He turned to face Karlene. "Karlene, I want to get dressed. This has gone too far. I knew I'd made a mistake putting you two together." He shivered; it was warm in the room. "Karlene is a bad influence and you're easily led."

"Yes, of course I'm a bad influence," Karlene said. She grinned, this was going well. "But Gemma is not easily led. This is what she wants, naughty sissy. You have a sexy dominant wife and home and yet you went to see professional mistresses. Tut tut."

Gemma's face was full of affection for her husband. She stroked his erection slow and gentle. Her face glowed with kindness and love. He looked confused. The two women glanced at each other and back at Paul.

"Be a good sissy, Pansy. Wait here." Karlene pointed to the spot where he was standing.

"I'll go to get your clothes for the evening." She watched him for a long moment. "You're going to look so pretty."

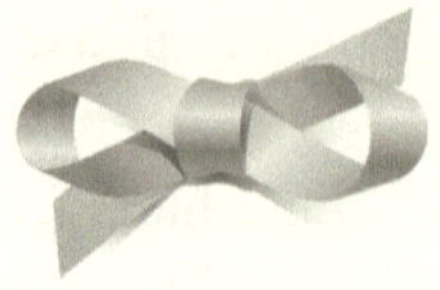

4 — Depilation

Karlene returned to the living room, she held a white electric razor with the cord trailing. She carried pink clothing over the other arm, a pair of large white sandals dangled from her fingers and a wide happy expression covered her face.

"You think I believed that silly story that you sometimes shaved to look good in the gym. Ha. You shaved for the mistresses, Pansy. And now we're going to shave everything below your neck sissy boy."

Paul's eyes shot away from Gemma and over to Karlene's tall lithe body as she approached him. Her voluminous breasts spilled out of the tight bra, large, smooth and inviting. And untouchable. Karlene placed the clothes on the sofa in a small folded pile. She placed a small black suitcase box next to them. On the top of the pile of clothes were a pair of panties in shocking pink. Beneath them was a matching bra. Karlene saw Paul look at the lingerie with a lustful expression.

Paul stood motionless while Gemma flicked at the end of his little straining erection with a single fingernail. She stopped and held it up with one fingernail as she told him how cute it was. "It's pretty and feminine. A little girl's clitty."

"And far too hairy." Karlene looked over his body. She rubbed her fingers together as if touching something dirty. Gemma led Paul with a hand gripped on his genitals. Karlene pushed the start button and the razor buzzed like a bee collecting pollen on a warm summer day. She pressed it to Paul's leg and circled up and down.

For a moment he didn't react. He tried to pull away. "What?" He said.

"Shush dear," Gemma whispered, her hand tightening on his balls. "I can squeeze harder if you struggle, Pansy dear."

"Is this part of the threesome sex game?" His voice trembled, his eyes dreamy.

"Sex game?" Gemma asked.

"Yes it's part of the sex game," Karlene cut in. "Just relax and enjoy." She shaved his legs and arms and chest. Short dark hairs covered his feet and the light carpet around him in a small circle. She moved to his balls. He pulled back.

Gemma's fingernails dug harder into his balls and his eyes watered. "Let Karlene shave your little bits, sweetheart. Or I'll be squeezing your little sissy plums a whole lot harder."

Karlene shaved his balls, penis and pubes clean.

Gemma led him back to the sofa and he remained compliant, caught between pleasure and a feeling this was so wrong. Karlene picked up the shocking pink panties and stretched them out in front of his face. They were like a small pair of shorts but made of fine see-through cotton. A tiny white frill ran outlined the legs and the top of the tiny panties. A small red bow was on the front.

Karlene knelt on the floor and lifted one of Paul's feet, her hand held his ankle with a light gentle grip. Gemma wrapped her hand around his little dick, holding it loosely, she rubbed a thumb along the top lovingly, absent-mindedly. His face was soft and sexual.

"Let me do it, Karlene," Gemma said with a soft tone.

The two ladies' gentle approach had lulled Paul into a lack of awareness of what was happening. He still thought this was going to be a threesome.

Karlene stood, a look of success at Gemma's enthusiasm at their task. "Of course."

Gemma took the pink panties from Karlene and hunched down and put her slim hand on Paul's calf. "Lift your leg, honey," she said as if putting girl's panties on her husband was a normal occurrence.

Paul looked at her, bemused. He allowed her to lift his leg. She slipped the panties over then pulled his foot to the floor. "Other leg, sweetheart," she said, her voice caring and loving. She rubbed a hand over his now smooth legs. "These are so smooth and feminine, petal. Like the good sissy boy you are."

Her soft words hypnotised Paul and he did what she said without argument. Gemma drew the panties up his legs, her long nails teasing against his shaved skin as she raised them over his knees. Karlene hadn't expected him to be so compliant, Gemma's affectionate approach had subdued any fight he may have had.

She tugged the panties up to his little balls and erect dick. The pink frilly waistband snagged underneath his erection.

"Let me help." Karlene lent in and poked it inside the elastic frill then cupped her hand around his balls and tucked them inside too. Her eyes twinkled at Gemma. "Teamwork," she said.

Paul remained in a delightful daze as Gemma tugged the panties up tight and stood back to take in her husband in panties. The panties were tight around Pansy's genitals and bum. A small lump protruded at the front and a small rounded shape hung below it. Otherwise, the fit looked feminine.

Karlene put a hand on his hip and inspected his behind. The panties half-covered his bum cheeks. The bottom half of his pale bum cheeks looked as if they had never seen the sun. Soft pink enveloped the top half of his cheeks, dots of pale skin showed through the tiny gaps between the fabric.

Pansy looked down then up. "Yes they are pretty, but why have you put these on me?"

Karlene looked surprised. "Because you're a sissy femboy, Pansy."

His mouth opened and shut. He didn't know what was going on but somehow loved everything they were doing. Karlene saw the confusion written on his face. Was this a fun sex game? Or something else. The two women were being gentle with him, but were they being nice to him? He was about to find out.

Gemma put her arms around him from behind. She pressed her boobs into his back. Her hand went down to his erection and she ran her hand over it through his panties. "These are sexy, sissy sweetheart."

Paul continued to revel in the attention and let the ladies do what they wished. For now. Karlene noted the loving approach was working well. Gemma was being genuine, she loved him. For Karlene, it was a tactic she noted for the future. Even an experienced dominatrix can still learn new tricks.

Karlene passed Gemma the matching pink bra. She pulled it around Paul's chest. Gemma had provided Karlene with his measurements. He remained transfixed by their attention. Karlene put a hand on his erection through the panties and cupped it and his little balls, kneading them like soft dough balls. Paul gasped in pleasure.

Gemma attached the bra clasp against her husband's back, her fingers twisting the small clasps into the hooks. She ran a hand down his back, over the bra strap and to his bottom. She grabbed a panty filled cheek in one hand and squeezed and pinched it. The panties were like a pink skin over his firm bottom cheeks.

Gemma joined Karlene facing him and they perused Paul's appearance. His panties moulded themselves around his little erection, the shape clear. His small almond-like balls outlined the tight material, like the lips of a vagina.

Paul came out of his trance at that moment. "What have you done?" A sharp touch of anger in his voice but it seemed faked.

Gemma hugged him. "You look so lovely, my pretty princess."

"Princess?" He complained, but made no move to push his wife away.

Gemma nuzzled his neck, her hands swimming over his bum cheeks feeling the soft panties.

Karlene picked up a powder-pink dress. "Time for the pretty dress." He looked and let out a long burst of breath.

Gemma untangled herself from Paul.

Karlene held the dress up to him, placing it against his shoulders. It covered the top half of his pink panties, the small bulge showed. He looked down at it in horror and utter desire and tried to move back. Gemma held his arm, digging her fingers in. He stopped. His pretence at hating this was clear.

Karlene grabbed at his balls. She tightened. He winced, a tear formed in both eyes and dripped from the corners, sliding down each cheek. Karlene wasn't sure if it was from his humiliation or the pressure she maintained on his balls. Maybe both. She tightened and twisted.

"It's time for you to become my pretty Pansy Princess." She squeezed his balls harder and he grimaced. "We're going to dress you up as the sissy femboy you are. I've never seen you dressed like a sissy, unlike the Mistresses you paid. Imagine that. Keeping it from your wife. How could you? You're going to be my Pansy because you're not a man, you're a sissy femboy." Gemma planted a soft kiss on his bemused lips. "Won't that be fun, Pansy? And you know I love you, especially as a sissy boy."

He shook his head. "Gemma, honey, what are you doing?" He turned to Karlene. "What have you done to my wife?"

Karlene opened up the rear zip of the sissy dress. "I reminded Gemma she was a stunning Goddess and that you are a pansy princess. Nothing she didn't know, she just needed reminding. Oh, I did tell her you'd called me wanting me to be your mistress and feminise you into a pansy princess." She held the dress above his head. "Hands up, sissy. You got your wish."

"I will not," he said.

Gemma let go of his arm and slid her hand down to his erection, keeping her face close to his. She kissed his cheek again and grabbed his balls through the panties, squeezing them. Her fingers pressed into the soft delicate sacks and touched her fingertips against his inner sacks, not wanting to hurt him. Too much. Not yet.

"Hands up Pansy, like Karlene asked you nicely. Or do you want your Goddess Gemma to squeeze these little sissy sacks a little harder?"

Gemma's fingers dug into his balls. He let out a squeal. Her hand tightened and he held his breath. He raised his hands and Gemma smiled and kissed him with a light brush of her lips.

"Good girl."

Karlene pulled the powder pink cotton dress over his head and tugged on in. It sat perfectly on his shoulders, it had a flat white collar and short puffed sleeves. Paul looked down at his chest and read the writing on the front.

Little Princess

"And that's what you are," Gemma said. "My little pansy princess." She tweaked his cheek with her thumb and forefinger. "My good little *cutey-wutey* pansy in a *cutey-wutey* little girl's party dress." Gemma screwed up her nose and eyes in a kind smile.

His face bloomed into a deep magenta shade. "I don't want to wear this stupid dress, I feel silly, Gemma. What are you doing? Is this some kind of prank?"

"Well, you seemed to want to wear dresses like this with professional Mistresses," said Gemma.

Karlene tweaked his erection hard with a finger and thumb. He groaned "Ow."

"Pansy-wansy doesn't want her *pwitty* party *dwess*?" She tweaked harder. "What do you think a pansy sissy should wear? A male suit, long grey trousers and black shoes?" She looked him in the eye and laughed once. "No, a pansy princess like you should always wear pretty pansy party dresses."

He looked to the floor, his face glowed hot with shame and a strange comfort and pleasure. A shiver shot through him. His body trembled, a tear of shame and delight came to the corner of each eye.

"There's a good sissy femboy, let the tears come. Sissy-girls cry, there's nothing to be ashamed of." Karlene said.

She knelt and picked two white socks from the clothes pile. She pushed them onto both feet. They finished at his ankle in pink frills. Karlene rubbed her hand up his smooth white leg.

"The other sissies are going to love you looking pretty and enchanting in your pansy princess dress."

Paul' tried to say something. Gemma put an ear to his mouth. "Don't be shy Pansy, tell us."

"What other sissies, what are you talking about?" His voice was low and raspy.

Karlene's hands went to his girly balls and she stroked them lovingly through his panties. Gemma's hand touched the front of his panties, his erection, and rubbed over it. Karlene's other hand stroked his hair.

"You're a sissy-femboy and other sissies are going to love you. Quite literally." Karlene let go of him and picked up the sandals. She pushed them on his feet. She did up the straps while Gemma kept him calm caressing his erection through the panties. She stopped as soon as he seemed on the brink of cumming. She looked at him with a wide engaging smile.

"No making a sissy mess, you naughty pansy." She slapped his erection playfully. Then she slapped it again and giggled each time. "It's such a cute little miss clitty, so pretty covered in pink girly panties." She looked at him with love. "I want to squish it up." She twisted and pulled on it, her face full of love. And mischief. He squealed in joy and hate.

Karlene pushed his feet into the sandals and buckled up the straps.

Gemma said. "Pretty shoes for a pretty pansy."

Karlene picked up a pink Alice band with a small pink bow attached to the top. She slid it into his hair. Paul put his hands to his head and squealed, "No."

Gemma took his hands gently and rubbed them in hers. "Now, now sissy, calm down. We're making you as pretty as a pansy, I'm doing this for love. You know how much I love you, Pansy?"

He mumbled that he thought she did.

Gemma put on a face of fake disappointment. She slapped his cheek playfully then shook his erection with two fingers. "How can you doubt I love you, Princess? You know I do." She stroked his face. "Why else would I be doing this to do?"

He went to answer but couldn't think of what to say so shut his mouth again.

Karlene grabbed the side of his hair and pulled it into a four-inch-long pigtail. She flicked a pink band into the base. She repeated it on the other side while Gemma kept him docile by stroking his erection and whispering how she loved her pansy princess.

Karlene unclipped and opened the black miniature suitcase-like box. It was full of coloured eyeshadows, eyeliner pencils, tubes of face makeup and several tubes of lipstick.

Paul peered inside the box then looked up at his wife. He shook his head.

Gemma tapped him on the arm with a fist. "Silly Pansy Princess, don't be so shy. I know you want this. We're going to make you up like a pretty sissy femboy. What's the matter with you? Anyone would think you don't want to be a pansy princess, Petal."

He didn't get the chance to reply. Karlene picked up a wide brush and dabbed at tan-coloured make-up and dabbed it around his face. He moved his head away. Gemma squeezed hard on his genitals and held her hand in tight. He breathed in sharply.

"Don't struggle, Pansy, you know you want to look pretty for us. And for those pretty sissies, you're going to meet.

Paul's eyes widened with a mix of terror and wonder. Gemma let out her grip, but her hand remained tight around his balls. Karlene put the brush down and picked up a pencil. She flicked it against his eyelashes, making them darker and appear longer. She took a thin stick with a small pad on the end and dabbed it in a green eyeliner shade. She ran it over his eyelids and dabbed it in with another brush.

As she worked, Karlene said to Gemma, "Now you're Goddess Gemma, you need to be sexually satisfied by a real man as soon as possible. Pansy's little girly parts pale in comparison to those of the real men you're going to fuck. Even other sissies had bigger clitties than Pansy's little penis." They laughed.

Paul sniffled in worry. Karlene worked on his makeup. Gemma kissed his lips lightly, kneading his balls with light fingertips and he swooned. He shivered. "Please stop what you're doing." His pleading lacked conviction and he made no other effort to push them away.

Gemma stroked his balls. "I love you, Pansy, and I love that you're a sissy femboy with a tiny miss clitty."

Karlene picked up a lipstick in shocking bright red. "Pucker up, girly."

Gemma squeezed on his balls. He groaned and puckered his lips. Karlene spread the lipstick over his lips and told him to push his lips together. She showed him how. Karlene stood back and admired her work.

"I'd say she's ready, Gemma."

Anguish etched in Paul's face. His little side pigtails swung with his head movements, his little chiffon party dress swished and brushed around the tiny lump in his panties.

"Yes, she is," said Karlene. "And now we need to get ready too."

"Ready for what?" Paul's desperate voice was a tone higher than normal.

Karlene and Gemma smiled at him as a reply. Gemma grabbed his balls and pulled him towards the door, his face in despair.

"Follow me, Pansy Princess."

He had no choice, Gemma's hand was clamped tight around his little balls. He had no idea what was waiting for him next. He knew it would be nothing he expected. And that surprise shot a jolt of electricity from his stomach to his throat.

5 — Sissy Princess

Gemma led Paul up the stairs by an ear and into the master bedroom. Karlene was in front and glanced back several times, aware Pansy was watching her bare arse wiggle. That was good, it increased his desire and desperation. These were the tools she used to control sissies and make them do her bidding.

They entered Paul and Gemma's marital bedroom. Gemma dropped hold of his ear absent-mindedly. Karlene saw his little erection hard and strong through the panties. He had been erect for around an hour, he would be feeling desperate to cum. That was not going to happen.

Gemma looked him up and down, her innocent face alive with wonder. Her bra held the promise of for Paul but her nipples, somehow, remained inside the cups. The arced tops of her dark areola invited him, her rounded mounds were alluring. Paul's hand pushed out towards one of his wife's breasts, involuntarily, a reaction. Gemma swiped it away without breaking her innocent smile.

"Naughty, Pansy puff, no touching." Gemma's voice was smooth like velvet. Sissies mustn't touch Goddesses."

"You're my wife, Gemma." Paul fidgeted in discomfort. He crossed his legs, as if he wanted to pee.

Karlene's face carried a confident playful smile. "As Goddess Gemma said, sissy femboys don't touch goddesses." Karlene stared hard at him. He withered beneath her strong brown eyes and soft velvet voice.

"Mistress Karlene," Karlene said.

Incomprehension burned in his eyes, his body shivered with horny anticipation.

"You will call me Mistress Karlene. An... ur sexy wife is Goddess Gemma."

He mouthed a, "What?" He put out a han... wards Karlene. She batted it away.

"You will curtsey to us and apologise for trying to ...pe us. Say sorry Mistress Karlene and sorry Goddess Gemma. And I ...nt to see you holding out the sides of your dress, like a good sissy."

He was unable to speak, the situation he wa... in was uncomprehending. Half an hour ago he was pulling up in his driveway ready for a quiet night in watching TV with Gemma. Now he was in a little girl's dress and Karlene and Gemma were dominating him. OK, he had just been on the phone to a Mistress arranging something similar but even so. This was beyond weird. His wife and his ex-girlfriend working together.

A short moment elapsed as he didn't curtsey. Karlene lost patience. She slapped his face.

Paul gasped in shock, his eyes watered. Karlene twisted his ear.

"Curtsey, Pansy. If you do as I ask, I won't have to slap you again, will I?"

He didn't want any slapping. Or did he? He'd play along, at least he wasn't paying 200 an hour, this was free. His hands went to the sides of his dress. He held it out and curtsied. Exciting. He said, "Sorry Mistress Karlene, sorry Goddess, Goddess." He swallowed hard. Even so, this was not right. It was one thing paying a professional to do a job and feminise and humiliate him. There was something not quite right when it was your wife.

Karlene let go of his balls and wiped a hand on his dress with a disgusted face A small circular damp stain showed on his panties. "Yuk, pre-cum sissy juice. Naughty girl." A smile danced in Karlene's voice.

She turned back to Gemma. "Time to get ready."

"Ready for what" aul's voice was unsteady, nervous. And yet the suspense was exhila ng. It had to be something sissy and humiliating. How wonderful.

"We need t ok our best, especially that hot sexy goddess of a wife of yours." Kar e strode to a large fitted wardrobe. It ran the length of the wall.

Paul's es followed her. She opened the doors to reveal a row of elegant esses. His mouth dropped open. "That's my side of the wardrobe, where are my clothes?"

Gemma ran her finger down his cheek, finishing on his lips. "We've moved them, Pansy."

"Where to?"

The two ladies ignored his question.

One thing was coming after the other and he was struggling to keep up with what was happening to him. Karlene took out a sleek red dress with a low back. Gemma went to her side of the wardrobe and selected a hanger with a small burgundy cocktail dress.

Karlene slipped the red dress on. "Pansy girl, you've been hiding in your sissy closet for too long. No more skulking sissy."

Karlene walked to the other side of the bedroom and sat at Gemma's dressing table and peered in the mirror. She spoke as she applied make-up. "Your goddess of a wife needs a real man. She's suffered for too long having a husband who is nothing more than a girly pansy with a tiny clitty. We're going to rectify that problem this evening."

Karlene applied eyeshadow to her wide eyelids.

"Your goddess wife's new boyfriend will be arriving shortly. Apart from giving Gemma what she's been missing for three years, he will make you more of an obedient little girl for your wife. He will be good for you, Pansy, and teach you to be a well-behaved cuckold pansy princess."

Paul stood shivering by the end of the bed. She had to be joking. It was more of the game they were playing. It should have been perfect but he had a nagging doubt. Karlene sat on the end of the bed and reached out to his little erection. Gemma went to the dressing table to do her make-up.

Karlene stroked Pansy's erection with a single fingertip through his panties. "It's so cute, pansy-girl, especially wrapped up in pretty pink panties."

Pansy squeezed his eyes in frustration. Each time Karlene detected he was on the brink of orgasm, she withdrew her fingers and waited for him to calm down. She then started again. He sweated and flushed. "Please let me cum. I'm uncomfortable.

Karlene smiled and giggled at him. She stroked his clitty, stopped, let him calm down. She started again.

Gemma sat next to Karlene on the end of the bed. Gemma joined Karlene rubbing his erection through the panties. Gemma rubbed her fingers up and down his erection. Then stopped. Karlene took over, rubbing Pansy's erection. As he started to groan in anticipation of a release, she stopped. They waited for him to calm down, his almost orgasm waned. Gemma rubbed it again.

"We can't have you messing in your pretty panties, pansy," Karlene said.

"Little girl Pansy. Goddess Gemma needs a real man in bed."

"I need a real man," Gemma said. "You were such a little sissy femboy, Pansy. You cry and squeal like a baby girl during sex." Gemma's voice was caring, her voice demure and sexy.

The two ladies hunched their shoulders and giggled. Pansy tried to grope his wife. Karlene slapped his hand away.

"Please Gemma, please Karlene. I need to cum. I'm in agony, I'm bursting. I need to cum. It hurts." He knelt on the floor and put his hands together in prayer. Broken, desperate. "I beg you, Gemma."

Gemma pulled Pansy up by his armpits as he sobbed anguished tears. He attempted to touch her breast again, without thinking. He was desperate. Gemma pushed him away and kissed him on the lips. He stopped crying and she hugged him tight and let go suddenly.

Karlene stood and planted a kiss full on his lips, her tongue licked around his mouth. He was shocked and wiped his eyes. What were they doing? He tried to reach Karlene's breast and Gemma slapped his arm hard and he withdrew it looking hurt. He twisted in his white sandal shoes, ever more frantic.

Gemma slapped him hard twice across the face, Karlene looked on, eyebrows raised in mild surprise but pleased at Gemma's approach. Gemma was getting into her role as Goddess Gemma with relish.

Without warning, Gemma took his ear and twisted it hard. Pansy said, "Owwww." She took his other ear and twisted it the same way, pulling him down to bend in half.

She whispered sweet comments as she twisted his ears and slapped his face. "Poor Pansy, you're not a man. No. You're my girly princess with a tiny clitty and sissy balls." Her voice was honey-smooth and calm.

She slapped his face more rapidly. Not too hard but irritating. Pansy tried to put his arms up, like a boxer's defence, but Gemma switched between ear twists and face slaps. Karlene watched and wanted to join in the fun. She slapped up at his girly balls and pulled his little clitty hard.

Pansy he pleaded for them to stop, begged them to leave him alone. Light annoying slaps rained around his cheeks, Karlene hit at his balls. The women laughed and giggled.

Faster and faster the slaps come down on him. He twisted and turned from the two ladies' hands, his hands flapping in vain as if trying to swat fast mosquitoes. The first drops of tears appeared in the corners of his eyes. He whimpered. The tears trickled down his face against the red slap marks.

Karlene's face was alive. "She's becoming a real baby girl." She smiled at Gemma. "Your new hunky boyfriend is going to love her this way. A sobbing sissy."

6 — Sissy Fun

"I never imagined this would be such fun, Karlene. My sissy husband is a whining sissy femboy. It's delightful." Gemma's face was alive.

Karlene had Pansy's balls clamped tight in one hand. For a few wicked moments, she considered how it would be nice to snip them off completely. Then Pansy would be more like a real girl. That's probably a step too far. She parked the idea. Maybe in the future, let's see.

Karlene said, "I don't believe Pansy is crying properly; a few little tears isn't enough. If she's to become a proper little sissy we need to see lots more tears. Crying like a little girl."

They picked the pace up. The speed of their slaps increased. One-two, one-two. Faster and faster. Karlene's hand was so tight around his girly balls, she felt his inner ball sacks. His eyes were full of watery tears. How must Pansy feel, she wondered? His face winced.

She had an idea. She pulled his panties down to his knees, went to the dressing table and returned with a hair clip. She pressed it on the top of his balls like a clamp.

Karlene swiped against his erection. Again and again. One two, one two. Then again. And again. All the time, she spoke to Pansy, "*You're a sissy girl, a pansy princess. You're not a man, you're a femboy sissy. A sissy slut.*"

Her words worked to the beat of the swipes, their voices soft and gentle. There was a hint of laughter in their voices.

Whack, whack. Gemma's hands heated his cheeks with slaps. She moved on to his ears. Boxing them, twisting them. He didn't know where to turn. He didn't know what to protect. Two pairs of pretty elegant hands working him over. Two voices, loving, caring, taunting, insulting.

Soft voices, "You're a sissy pansy, you're a girly princess," over and over again and again. Scoffing, insulting. Their hands struck him as they spoke. Faster. Faster.

Pansy fell to her knees, head down, penis small and hard. Karlene stopped slapping and Gemma followed her lead. The room fell into silence. Pansy lifted her head and looked to the ceiling. He looked up at the two ladies with a forlorn face. Behind his eyes, a look of wonder sparkled.

Gemma stroked the back of his head. She soothed him and told him, "Let it out, Pansy. That she's a good girl, a poor pansy. Cry little girl tears." She stroked her chin and laughed at him through her fingers across her mouth.

She lifted him to his feet again by an ear. Pansy begged them, "Enough. Please. Stop teasing. I want to have sex with Gemma. It's gone on long enough."

"Karlene ran a single finger down her little girly dick, still hard despite the slaps and swipes. "Pansy wants sex with his hot goddess of a wife?"

"Yes, yes, yes please. Please."

The two ladies made a show of pretending to think about it. A moment later, Gemma slapped Pansy around the ears, left then right, left then right. As she hit him, Karlene took her girly dick and rubbed his foreskin, up and down, slowly with a soft light touch. They told him, "Sissy femboys don't have sex with their wives. You're an adorable princess, not a man. Does Pansy want to cum? Yes? Well you can't."

Pansy's shoulders slumped.

Karlene continued to rub his erection. "It's time."

Pansy looked up. "Time for what? Sex?"

"It's time we called your hot wife's new boyfriend and invited him over."

"Boyfriend? What are you talking about? You're kidding. It's part of this game?" His voice was desperate and strained.

"No game, Pansy." Karlene rummaged through her handbag. She pulled out her mobile phone and scrolled through her contacts. "Ah, here we are." She pressed on the contact and shifted her head to one side so that her hair moved away and she could tuck her phone to her ear. A faint ring tone buzzed.

"Your sexy wife's new boyfriend will help us to complete your transition into a cuckolded pansy princess."

Pansy tugged and wriggled in Gemma's grip without success. Karlene spoke into her phone, short and sharp. "Lily? Come now." She hung up. She re-dialled. "Hello Frank, come over now to the address I sent earlier." She hung up.

Karlene stroked his erection lightly as she spoke. "Frank is going to satisfy your wonderful goddess of a wife." Karlene nuzzled Pansy's nose with hers and sat back, her hand stroking his erection with a gentle flick. "And I have another friend for you, a friend to help you on your way to sissy-hood."

She thought for a moment, a finger on her chin.

"Sissy-hood? Is that even a word?"

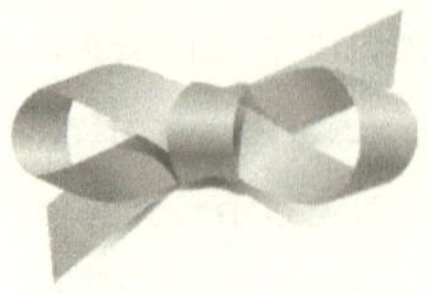

7 — Stud

Frank filled the door-frame of the master bedroom. 230lbs of muscle rippled. His shoulders and upper arms tensed against the taut cotton of a tight black tee-shirt. The dome of his shaved head shone like polished coal and black whiskers covered his head. The shadow of a beard looked like a tattoo around his square chiselled chin. His eyes were deep dark brown, as if looking down a long dark tunnel.

Frank had arrived a few minutes ago. Karlene watched as Gemma's eyes feasted over Frank's giant muscular frame. Her eyes dropped to the bulge in his crotch area and remained there. The memories of seeing what lay inside strong. He wore tight blue jeans on and a giant long sausage-like bulge was outlined down one leg.

Gemma held her husband in a headlock. Pansy's eyes shot up to the giant and then to the bulge in his trousers. He was sobbed a, "No, Gemma, no." He trembled like a chicken about to be plucked alive.

Frank nodded to Gemma and grunted in a baritone growl.

Gemma waved a hand at him and said, "Hello again, big boy." Her eyes remained fixed on the outline of his cock in his jeans.

Karlene pointed to Pansy under Gemma's elbow. "This is Goddess Gemma's sissy princess husband. We call her Pansy. She's the one I told you about, the pansy with the little dick who can't satisfy this beautiful Goddess."

Frank moved into the room and stood over them. Karlene ran a hand down his trouser bulge. "I' know you have something better than Pansy has to rectify the situation for Gemma."

"Yes," Frank boomed. His voice vibrated in the room like an aftershock

Gemma grabbed her husband's balls and held one arm behind Pansy's back. She forced her husband to curtsy for Daniel.

"Say hello, Sir, there's a good prissy pansy." She twisted Pansy's arm higher up his back.

Pansy looked up and mumbled, "Hello Sir."

The women giggled. Frank folded his massive arms and it looked as if his tee shirt sleeves might rip under the strain of his expanded biceps.

Karlene lifted Pansy's little erection head up with one finger. "Goddess Gemma has a problem, as you can see."

Frank guffawed at the sight of the erection, loud and deep.

"Pansy has serious problems in bed. As you can see, she's a sissy femboy who can't satisfy her wife. We need your assistance, Frank."

"Yes, Mistress Karlene." His voice boomed against the bedroom walls like thunder.

"Goddess Gemma needs a real man and new lover. You two will make a perfect couple; you're looking for a sexy new girlfriend and Goddess Gemma needs a real man." Karlene's face went serious. "Gemma still loves her sissy husband and he's perfect in every department except the single most important area. So she needs your help."

Karlene cupped under Pansy's tiny sissy balls.

"She has a tiny dick and balls," Frank said. His eyes lingered on Pansy's small erection and then he studied Gemma. "You are beautiful, Goddess Gemma, like Mistress Karlene."

"Why thank you, Frank, it's nice of you to say so." Karlene was surprised to see a blush on Gemma's face before she regained her composure. Gemma was fascinated by this giant hunk of testosterone standing inches from her.

"Gorgeous," Frank said. "Sexy." He stared at Gemma.

"Yes, thank you," said Karlene. "We get the picture. Enough talking. We're not here for your less-than-stimulating conversation but for your enormous penis."

Karlene took over the headlock on Pansy. Karlene slapped Pansy's ears. Gemma spanked his bottom. Frank watched, the two women enraptured by Daniel's stiffening cock outlined in his trouser leg

Pansy begged, "Please stop, please. Not in front of this man."

Gemma couldn't take her eyes from the erect cock outlined in Frank's trousers. She stopped spanking Pansy and placed a hand over the outline. She rubbed gently.

Pansy spotted her and froze. "Stop, no. What are you doing? You're married to me."

Karlene slapped his face and pulled hard on his balls.

Gemma smiled indulgently at her husband's plaintive pleas. Karlene kept Pansy in a headlock and turned him to face Gemma. His eyes widened in horror and seeing her squeezing Franks erection through the trousers. Gemma's hands ran up over his stomach and his biceps. She pulled Frank down onto the bed. He sat awkwardly with an expectant grin as Gemma peeled off his tee-shirt in a frenzy.

He had shaved his body and it looked like a statue. He took Gemma's face in both his hands and pulled her in for a long deep kiss. Pansy whined as Gemma closed her eyes.

Pansy remained held under Karlene's armlock, forced to watch, unable to look away. He called out, Stop, don't do this." Karlene walked Pansy round under her arm to position him to the side of Frank sitting on the bed.

Gemma stepped off the bed with a bounce, her dress flowing around her legs. She parted Frank's thick legs and kneeled on the floor between them.

"You're a hunk, Frank." Gemma fought with the top button on his jeans.

Frank put a hand on her head and a finger on her lips. "You're a stunning babe, Goddess Gemma. Sexy as hell."

Gemma managed the button and unzipped his flies. She pulled his jeans down to his knees with a desperate lunge.

"Gemma, no, it's not too late. Stop this." Pansy looked on fascinated and horrified.

Gemma saw his little penis remained hard and erect. He was getting off on this too. She looked back at Frank. She hadn't noticed he wasn't wearing underpants. His gigantic erection pointed up like a black steel girder, hard and threatening. Karlene held pansy and let him take in the sight of the eleven-inch erect cock. It was hovering close to Gemma's open and astonished lips.

Gemma removed his jeans, slid in close and took the erection in one hand as Pansy groaned. She looked all around and over it, savouring the sight of a real man's penis. She put a hand under his balls, looking over, around under with wonder. She sat back, fixed on the erection and the two massive sacks hanging between his legs.

Gemma came out of her surprise at the sight of the monster cock. She giggled. "Gosh, my husband is such a little sissy femboy compared to you." She puffed her cheeks out and blew. "In height and the size of your cock and your balls. My femboy husband is nothing more than a little pansy girl compared to a powerful hunk like you."

Frank grunted in pleasure. Pansy groaned. Karlene held Pansy's head up by his hair on the top of his head. She told him to watch how a real man performs.

Gemma stood over Franks, his erection touching her stomach. They kissed again. Tentative at first. Gemma's hand went to his thigh, he took her hand and guided it onto his cock. They kissed harder. Taking breaths, tongues lashing, then plunging deep into their mouths. Their lips were locked in passion. Frank pulled Gemma's dress straps down and they fell over her bra. She stood up and the dress fell off and to her feet. She kicked it away, sat next to Frank and took his erection in one hand. She worked her fist up and down it, her face in total wonder.

Pansy watched, he trembled. He squealed at what he was seeing, unbelieving. His wife was fondling and kissing another man. In front of him. This was the worst thing he'd ever witnessed. And the most stimulating, better even than when Karlene used to do it to him over ten years ago.

Karlene smirked. This was going better than she had anticipated. Now for the next event.

8 — Desire

Frank flicked open Gemma's bra with a single practised twist of his enormous thick fingers. Her large oval breasts spilled into his huge receptive hands. The darkness of his hands was like charcoal against her snow-white skin. He moved his head between her breast mounds, his wide thick lips spread against her breasts, ravishing them with his long thick tongue. Another grain from Pansy.

Gemma reached for her new boyfriend's strong erection, she squealed in delight at the size and hardness. Pansy squealed in horror at seeing his wife with another man's cock in her hand. Frank's cock was three times the size of Pansy's little maggot.

They lavished each other's open mouths, tongues licking and probing each other. They slurped on each other's tongues. Gemma put a hand on Frank's defined chest and moved back. He gave a small deep grunt of surprise. Gemma put her thumbs on either side of the waistband of her small panties. Frank grinned. She wiggled her bum four times and pulled the elastic down to her the top of her pubic mound. She stopped, tapped the end of his erection, pursed her lips and turned. Frank's face beamed, his eyes full of desire.

"No, please, Gemma, don't do this," Pansy pleaded, his eyes lapping in the event unfolding.

A loud slap from Karlene's hand sounded against the flesh of his bum cheek, silencing his whining.

Gemma wriggled her bottom cheeks into Frank's nose, he put his hands up to take her cheeks. His fingers dug into them as Gemma bent forward and wriggled her arse. She stood up and put her thumbs back in the waistband of her panties. She wriggled her behind twice more and pulled her panties down and let them drop to her ankles.

Karlene grinned and Pansy let out another stunted groan at seeing his wife's trimmed triangle of sandy pubic hair on show. Her labia's were open and inviting, the bud of her clitoris extended. She was damp. Pansy shook his head in silence, eyes pleading and desperate. He licked his lips. Karlene saw this wasn't so traumatic for him. She knew real sissies, like Pansy, enjoyed this humiliation. She was being kind to Pansy.

Gemma looked to Pansy. "Poor sissy. She can't have sex with her wife any more. Well, watch and see how a real man looks after your wife."

Gemma spun back to face Frank. She put her hands in her hair and swayed her hips, her pussy inches from his gurning face. He moved forward towards her sex, entranced by her as if a snake to a piper. As he was about to kiss her pubic hair, she put a hand on his forehead. She knelt and put her mouth to his ear. "Wait lover, I have something to do first."

She got on her knees and grabbed Frank's erect cock with a hand. Her mouth was open, ready. Another whine came from Pansy as she puckered her lips and planted a delicate kiss on the end of his cock.

Pansy sobbed a final. "*Nooooo.*"

Gemma ran her tongue on the head of the giant cock. Frank grinned like a schoolboy with candy. Gemma looked up at him and put her lips around the end. Her head moved down the wide black shaft, her blond hair falling on the tops of thick black muscular thighs.

Pansy's soft sobs and Gemma's slurps against the enormous cock were the only sound in the room. Her head came back up the end, they closed against the end and she opened wide. Her mouth slid down the long dark erection, her blond hair falling all around his crotch. She came back up, faster this time, a constant deep murmur of pleasure in her throat. Faster, her hand tight on the base of his cock.

"Look Pansy," Karlene instructed. "You hot wife is enjoying a real cock and a real man." She pulled on Pansy's neck with her armlock jerking him to see his wife in action. Pansy sobbed and pleaded, "No,

Gemma, no. Please, no." His eyes told a different story, excitement, lust, humiliating pleasure.

Gemma's mouth moved faster, taking his erection as deep as possible then back up, back down to her throat, then back up. Frank looked to the ceiling and grabbed the sheets around him. He tensed and jerked. A long guttural moan came from somewhere deep in his throat. He jerked again.

Gemma slowed, her mouth coming up to the end of his cock as thick cum oozed from the end and glooped down his shaft and from her mouth. She swallowed it in. Sucked and swallowed. He jerked and jerked again. She sucked like a giant black straw in a milkshake. She turned to the side to face her sissy husband who watched in absolute horror. Gemma smiled sweetly, large drops of Frank's viscous cum smeared over her face. She wiped a finger over it and popped it in her mouth. She closed her lips and swallowed. Her face lit up.

Gemma faced her pansy husband, her eyes gentle and unblinking, a faint creased smile on the edges of her eyes. "Frank, you're such a fantastic alpha hunk of a stud. I'd forgotten how it was to blow a real cock, the feeling of so much cum gushing into my mouth. My sissy princess of a husband is a silly pansy with a tiny little girl's clitty. I never imagined the ecstasy I was missing out on being with a real man."

Gemma climbed onto the bed and lay her head on a pillow. "I'm all yours, my hunky boyfriend. Do what your best, I know you will."

She lay back and spread her legs wide, her knees up, her feet on the sheets. Her damp vagina lips parted like a zipper coming undone. Frank moved his head between her legs. His big tongue lashed out and into her vagina. He licked her labia, she arched her back then slumped to the mattress again. Frank took her hips, his arms like those of a giant against Gemma's slim body.

Karlene pulled Pansy around to the side of the bed and pushed his face to look over his wife's open vagina as Frank's tongue licked all over it. Pansy's quiet tears dripped onto the white sheets. Karlene noted with satisfaction that despite the tears and protestations, Pansy's erection was stronger than ever. He was loving this. And not paying for the pleasure.

Frank worked his tongue in and out of Gemma's vagina, her wide open inviting hole. He found the bud of her clitoris and Gemma arched her back in ecstasy again and again. She moaned and screamed, "Yes, yes, yes, lover." She slumped back on the bed.

"Oh Frank," she said. "You're such a stud. I can't believe this. I love it." her voice was alive with the sensations of her orgasm. She sat up and he faced her. They cuddled and hugged then resumed their deep passionate kissing. As they snogged, Frank's cock hardened. That was amazing, such a stud, though Gemma. Soon it was full-on eleven-inch of hard firm tissue and engorged blood.

Gemma guided him to lay on top of her.

"Watch this Pansy-Princess," Karlene said

"Gemma, no. Not that. He isn't using a condom. Think about it. You're not taking any protection."

Two slaps from Karlene silenced Pansy.

Gemma took Frank's erection in one hand and guided it into her waiting warm vagina. He pushed it in, further, further. All the way to the hilt. She gasped and her eyes widened like dinner plates. "Oh Karlene, you won't believe this," she cried.

"I think I would, darling. I had him last week." She sniffed. "Not much up going on up top, I suspect all his blood is needed for his cock."

Gemma wasn't listening as Frank's pounding sped up, pushing in and out. He stopped and turned Gemma over, laying her face down. He pushed his straining erection into her vagina from behind and lowered himself down.

Gemma called out. "Oh yes, oh yes. Harder, faster my stud."

Pansy moaned and Frank pounded at her, his body slapping against her rounded bottom cheeks. He stopped, turned her around, and picked her up and got off the bed, locked together. Gemma wrapped her legs around his waist and the two moved together. Frank's erection moved in and out, more slowly, Gemma's head lolled back, she gave out groans and moans of delight. He moved faster. He carried her to a wall and pushed her up against it, still pounding, her feet were off the ground. Gemma's face was intense lust. Pansy cried out and squealed.

Frank and Gemma seemed to seize up as they stopped and cried out in unison. He pumped her once more, then stopped, his body wrenched in pleasure. He put Gemma down and let his cock fall out of her, rubbing it with a massive hand. It spurted up her stomach and to her breast. She rubbed it in and licked her fingers with a gleeful smirk.

They fell into each other's arms. They hugged for several seconds, calming down and feeling their affection. After several seconds, Gemma took her boyfriend's hand and guided him to the bed. They fell on their backs on the side, their feet on the floor. Daniel's penis laid long and limp on the top of his thigh, a drip of cum trickled along and down the side. A pool of his cum glistened on Gemma's stomach and over her breasts.

"Clean up time, Pansy." Karlene let go of his neck and pushed him towards the recovering lovers.

Pansy cringed, his face screwed up. He shook his head, his lips held closed.

"Yes, clean up, Pansy. This is your sissy role now."

Karlene pushed a wipe into his hand. "Clean them both up, Pansy."

Pansy tried to pull away. Karlene held him tight.

"Clean it all away like a good sissy."

Gemma and Frank propped themselves up on their elbows, breathing heavily, bathed in sweat to watch. Karlene's hand held Pansy's hair. Pansy shivered in disgust as he wiped away Daniel's cum which was smeared over his wife's body. Karlene spanked his bottom to hurry him along.

Gemma giggled the whole time.

Karlene pulled him to Frank and pushed him towards his long limp penis.

"Wipe it clean, Pansy. This is your job now, cleaning up after your hot wife and boyfriend have had frantic sex." She passed him a fresh wipe.

Pansy grimaced and wiped Frank's penis with a look of disgust creasing his face.

Karlene let Pansy stand up. His short pink princess dress was ruffled around his waist. His hair was pulled back by an Alice band with a large bow on top, two side pigtails moved as he walked.

Pansy's head dropped in a sign he wanted the night to finish. Meanwhile, Gemma was saying something to Frank. He grunted in agreement. Gemma sat up. "I have three announcements to make."

9 — Cuckold

Gemma remained naked, she was unconcerned, enjoying the recklessness and sexual freedom. She sat next to Frank on the edge of the bed. His expended cock lay lifeless on his leg. For now. Pansy's face was cut with anguish. It had to be over now.

"Firstly, I want to thank Karlene for introducing me to Frank."

Karlene bowed and laughed with Gemma. Daniel clapped twice.

"Secondly, I want Frank to be my boyfriend. I want more of what I just had. Wow. I know it's all a little rapid, but I've never experienced such sex. Ever. He will be the man of the house when he's here and sleep with me in the master bedroom. He is the only man here." She looked to the distressed Pansy.

"Finally, Pansy here." She pointed a sharp red fingernail at Pansy. "She will be our sissy servant and obedient femboy maid." Gemma leant over and stroked Pansy's head. "Did you see the lovely way she cleaned up Frank's cum? So cute I could squeeze her." She tweaked his cheek.

As her audience digested her words, she got up, picked up her discarded dress and slipped it on over her head. She handed Frank his jeans. She blew out slowly digesting what she'd just done. She took Pansy's hand. "I have something to show you Pansy darling. You're going to love this."

Pansy looked around, trying to take in the scene and what was happening. It was a blur of shocks.

Gemma led Pansy out of the master bedroom. She held his hand and took him past the family bathroom and to the end of the corridor. Karlene followed with Frank. He hadn't bothered to put his tee-shirt on and his muscles rippled as he walked.

A strong smell of fresh emulsion hit them at the end of the passage. Gemma pushed the door open on what had once been the small rear spare room. It was too small for a guest bedroom so they had used it for dumping things they didn't know what to do with.

Gemma walked through the door and the fresh paint smell became stronger. Sitting on the bed was a slim blond-haired girl. Her hair was straightened and fell down her back to her tiny waist. Her lips were painted bright pink, her nails were long and in the same pink colour. She wore a short pink pleated skirt with white stockings. The tops of her stockings showed on her thin white thighs. White suspender straps were clipped to the stocking tops. She wore four-inch thin high heels. Her skirt fell between her legs and around a small bulge.

Everyone squeezed into the small room. Pansy's face dropped like melting snow in the sun. Gemma waved an arm in the air. "Say hello to Lily, Pansy." Karlene spoke from the hallway. "She'll be your girlfriend. It's only fair. Your wife has a hot new boyfriend and you have a sweet sissy girlfriend."

Lily smiled demurely at Pansy and put out a wide hand to greet him. Pansy looked at her hand as if it were dog shit.

The room's walls were in powder-pink emulsion with brilliant white skirting boards and door frame. The single white bed had a dark pink headboard in crushed velvet. A pink pillow with frills around the edge had a cartoon picture of a princess on it from a recent movie. The bedspread had a similar picture. Several cushions in shades of pink were scattered around the bed, mixed with soft toys and dolls. Boy-band posters hung on the walls. Two three-foot-high posters of young naked men were also fixed to the wall, their huge cocks displayed with pride. Two had large erections.

"I had it redecorated today, for you Pansy." Gemma was pleased. "This is your new bedroom. You'll be sharing it with Lily when she comes to stay. Frank and I will be using the master bedroom. This is a little girl's room for my Pansy princess."

Pansy choked. Gemma put an arm around Frank, his face inexpressive. Karlene pulled Pansy to the bed by an ear and made him sit next to Lily. Lily's face gave nothing away, but they all spotted movement in the bulge under her skirt.

"Let me see you being demure and girly, Pansy."

Karlene squeezed against his little balls. Pansy complained. Karlene squeezed harder. "I want to see demure, girly. Flutter your eyelashes at Lily, look up with your chin down. And tell us how pleased you are to see Lily and how pretty she is." She squeezed hard and Pansy jumped. Pansy looked down and batted her eyelashes. "You're very pretty Lily."

Lily blushed and looked down, her hands between her knees.

"I'm pleased to hear you find Lily pretty, Pansy," Karlene said. "Since you think she's so attractive, you can be nice and hug her."

Pansy dropped his demure look. Karlene re-tightened her grip on his balls. Pansy shot his arms around Lily who looked surprised for an instant.

"Now kiss Lily on his lips. You two are going to become very close friends, if you know what I mean. And we'll watch when you do."

Lily puckered her mouth in preparation and closed her eyes. Her bulge popped out from below the short hem of her pink skirt, fully erect. Lily's clitty was nothing like Pansy's, it was at least eight inches. Pansy froze at the sight of it.

"Let's see those tongues working, sissies."

Karlene pushed Pansy's head towards Lily's. Their lips touched, Lily brushed her hair from her face and a long wide tongue deep into Pansy's mouth. Pansy choked.

Karlene's face went in close to Pansy's. "And what happened to your tongue, princess? Be loving with Lily."

Pansy poked her tongue out and touched on Lily's writhing tongue. Pansy pulled it back out as if he had been burned. Lily's lips encircled it and she sucked on it. Pansy's eyes went wide in terror.

"Excellent," Karlene said. "Now stand and face each other.

Lily and Pansy got off the bed and stood facing each other. Lily was around four inches taller than Pansy in her heels. The two ladies laughed. Frank watched without expression.

Karlene pulled a tape measure out. She knelt by Pansy and ripped her panties to the floor. She pulled on his little hard clitty. "Don't tell me you're not excited, pansy Princess. You're erect from kissing pretty Lilly and standing so close to her large clitty."

She ran her tape measure over his erection. She put a finger on the point on the tape that had come to the end. "Four inches, if I'm being generous." She stroked his erection under his dress. "It's so cute, so girly. I hope Lily is not as disappointed as Goddess Gemma was."

Lily smiled demurely and shook her head.

Gemma took Pansy's hand in both hers and rubbed lovingly on his palm and the back of his hand. "Now be a good girl and hold Lily's nice clitty."

Pansy tried to step back. Karlene held her. Lily's skirt rested on the top of her erection. Gemma prised opened Pansy's fingers and placed them on Lily' hard penis. She compressed his fingers around it. Lily's face broke into a broad smile.

"Good Pansy-girl. It feels nice, yes?"

Pansy grunted a reply.

"No, not good enough, Pansy Princess, dear. Tell us how sexy Lily's clitty feels, how you love touching another sissy's clitty. You're a pansy princess who wants a huge clitty in her sissy vagina and mouth. I know you want to drink Lily's sissy juice."

"But I don't." Pansy objected.

Gemma swiped her face and the his balls. "Not good enough, Princess." Her voice purred: sexy, coy and loving.

Pansy cleared his throat, he looked to the floor. "I love touching Lily's clitty and I want it in my mouth." Pansy's voice trailed off.

Gemma stroked Pansy's clitty and then his face, softly with care. "That's so sweet, Princess, I'm pleased to hear you say that."

She thought for a moment.

"Let's make your wish come true, shall we Pansy?"

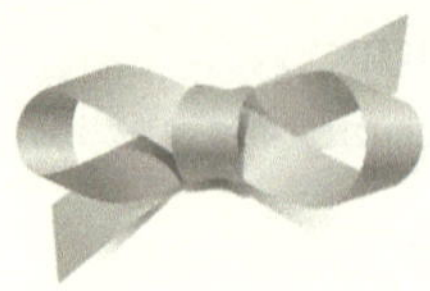

10 — Good Pansy

Gemma guided Pansy to his knees. Lily's clitty-penis stood firm and strong and aimed between his eyes. Pansy couldn't take his eyes of it. Threatening and promising. Horrifying yet tantalising.

Karlene gave Pansy the tape measure. "You will measure it and tell us how big it is."

Pansy's hands shook as she placed the yellow tape along the length of Lily's erection. He held a thumb at the end of the tape and squinted. "Eight inches. And a bit, Mistress Karlene."

"Eight inches and a bit?" Karlene said. "And yours is?"

Pansy's head dropped and arms fell to his side. He already knew his length as did Karlene, she'd measured it ten years ago when comparing it to the cocks of her lovers. "Three inches."

The two ladies giggled. "Three inches hard. A five-inch difference," Karlene stated.

Gemma took Pansy's hands and ran her fingers through them. "Which confirms that you, Pansy, are indeed a girly femboy." Her voice was smooth and controlled. Gentle and bewitching as she played with Pansy's fingers.

Pansy appeared to forget his predicament for a moment, entranced by his wife's loving voice and her hands and fingers around his. Gemma guided Pansy's hand to Lily's clitty. Pansy broke out of his daydream. Oh no, he was touching a male penis. He tried to pull his hand away, he wasn't gay. Gemma wrapped his fingers tighter around Lily's erection and held his hand firmly. She pushed Pansy's hands up and down the shaft as Lily mumbled a gentle sound. She took his hands and moved them to Lily's balls.

"This is how big male balls should be, Princess." Her hand remained over Pansy's hand, kneading and squeezing Lily's sacks. "Tell me how much you love Lily's sexy pussy balls, Princess." Their hands ran over them, Gemma pushed his fingertips into them."Or would you like me to squeeze on your pussy balls much harder than you're doing to your sissy girlfriend?"

Pansy choked and cleared his throat. "Yes, I love Lily's pussy balls." Pansy's voice was flat and emotionless.

"Good girl, good girl. I don't know if you're a gay femboy or a proper girl. It's becoming confusing." Gemma's voice was a hushed laugh.

"Turn and bend over, Lily." Karlene's voice was a gentle instruction.

Lily complied with evident pleasure, her round bare bottom faced Pansy, two balls hung, a blinking anus beckoned. Lily's bottom was inches from Pansy's horrified face. Gemma took one of Pansy's ears and guided her face to Lily's sissy vagina.

"Put your tongue out and lick around and inside Lily's nice vagina, there's a good sissy boy."

Pansy's tongue came out with a show of reluctance. Gemma twisted his ear harder and he shot it into the hole.

"Good sissy, now in and out and lick all around it."

Pansy complied, his eyes screwed up tight, his nose creased. Lily groaned with pleasure and circled her bottom in his face.

"And now her pussy balls, suck on the skin, Pansy Princess," Gemma ordered.

She tweaked Pansy's ear hard and pushed him deeper between Lily's legs to locate her long hanging pussy balls. They hung soft and smooth. Pansy's lips sucked the sack into his mouth, slurping. Gemma put her hand around Lily's balls and pulled them further into Pansy's mouth until it was full and he mumbled incoherently in some kind of complaint.

Gemma tugged Pansy's head back by a pigtail. "Now tell Lily how much you love her pussy balls and how big and tasty they are. Then tell us all how much you love to see Sir satisfy your hot sexy wife." Gemma's voice was soft and gentle. "That would be me, Pansy, your hot sexy wife who you failed to satisfy with your missy clitty."

She pulled his ear hard, Pansy screamed a stifled complaint.

"I love your sexy pussy balls, Lily." Pansy's voice was erratic, breaking, on the verge of breaking into floods of tears.

"And the rest, Pansy-puff." Gemma looked at Karlene and said gently. "This is wonderful."

"I love when you satisfy my hot wife, Sir." Pansy's mouth tightened.

"OK, it's time," Karlene said.

Pansy looked at her with intense apprehension in his eyes.

"Sit on the edge of Pansy's little single bed, Lily," said Karlene, "and open your legs as wide as possible."

Lily sat. She pushed her skirt up to reveal the massive erection. It was large, throbbing and proud.

Gemma pulled Pansy up by an ear and pushed him between Lily's legs. She put her hands on either side of Pansy's face and pushed it down to touch the underside of Lily's erection. She pulled Lily's large erect clitty and placed it to Pansy's closed lips.

"Open wide, Princess, this is what you want. You're a gay femboy and you know in your heart this is what you always wanted."

She tapped Pansy's lips and then prised opened his mouth. She pushed the erection deep into Pansy's mouth. She pressed against the back of his head and Pansy took the entire length in.

"Close your lips around it and I want you to move gently up and down, like the girly sissy you are."

Pansy followed his wife's order, his face a picture of anguish. His eyes sparking with something else. Gemma held the side of his head and guided Pansy's mouth up and down the erect shaft. Lily breathed faster, her mouth open, her eyes closed, her head back. Her blond hair fell to the bed behind her back. Gemma moved Pansy's falsely reluctant mouth more rapidly, up and down. Pansy's lips glided over the veins in Lily's erection which was bursting and brimming. Lily gave out a loud sound and her body shook. Pansy tried to take his mouth away, her face creased in horror, cringing in disgust. Gemma put a hand on Pansy's chin, the other on the top of his head.

"Swallow the nice sissy juice, Princess. You're going to adore the taste."

She held his nose and he swallowed. Then again. Again. Lily laid back. She spurted more timed and eventually, her flaccid clitty fell from Pansy's cum filled mouth. A line of white cum trailed away, joining Pansy's mouth with the tip of Lily's clitty-penis. Lily's breathing became more shallow as she calmed.

Gemma pulled Pansy's mouth over the end of Lily's flaccid clitty. "Every drop, sissy-boy. Clean it all up like a good femboy."

Pansy licked away the last stringy drops of Lily's viscous juices.

"Good sissy boy, see how much you love playing with Lily," Karlene said. "It's sissy love for sure."

Karlene pushed Pansy to lay beside the now dozy feeling Lily. Pansy laid back, his body and arms stiff, distaste fixed on his face.

Gemma sat on the bed at their feet. "Lily, darling?"

Lily opened one eye, long black false eyelashes batted.

"Would you be a dear for me? I know you're tired but be a dear and take my sissy husband's sissy virginity. I know you've just cum, but I'm sure you can manage one more time. Karlene tells me you're a wonder at recovery."

Lily sat up with a weariness and a weakly wicked grin. Pansy's face was full of apprehension once more. Gemma tipped Pansy over and lifted his dress up to expose his small pert bottom. Gemma put her hands under her sissy husband's body and told him to get on all fours. Lily moved behind Pansy without instruction. Karlene had trained her well.

Lily's clitty-penis hung limp. Gemma rubbed gel over it and then rubbed it up and down with gentle lithe fingers. She leaned over and licked and sucked around the end, her tongue flicked out, probing the end. Lily's penis slowly came back to full attention. Gemma stepped back, admiring her handy work and the sight of this sissy's full erection. Lily was so feminine, but with a large smooth yet very male appendage.

Gemma took the base of Lily's erect clitty in her hand and steered it to touch against her sissy husband's open and ready sissy vagina. Pansy flinched. Gemma licked her finger and wiped it around the end of Lily's clitty head.

"Go," she said,

Lily pushed slow and gentle and it popped in. She pushed gently until she had Pansy impaled up to the hilt of her erection. Pansy squealed once but a soft look appeared across his face as if in a different world. Lily placed her hands on either side of Pansy's hips and withdrew her hard clitty almost to the end. She thrust it in, all the way, faster this time with a little more force. Her smooth pubic area pressed against Pansy's behind. She pulled it to the end again then thrust in, long and deep. Pansy groaned and squealed, this time from pleasure. Lily moved faster. Deep then out, deep, then out.

Lily exploded into Pansy without warning, three, four jerks. She flopped onto Pansy's back. White-grey sissy juices oozed from Pansy's sissy vagina and dripped down his leg. He also flopped onto his side, exhausted from the pleasure yet still with an urge to cum.

Karlene took Lily's hand. "Up you get, that was a good performance. You've been a good sissy." Lily grinned, her eyes drooping with tiredness.

Pansy turned over, he put a hand to his bottom cheeks. Whether it was the pain of humiliation or the pleasure of having had an enormous erect cock in her anus for the first time, Karlene wasn't sure. Possibly both.

"Come on sissies, time for bed, sleep time for the two femboy princesses." Gemma stroked Pansy's forehead lovingly.

"Can't I come and sleep with you, Gemma?" he asked.

Gemma smiled an indulgent smile. "Silly sissy, pansy princesses don't sleep with goddess wives. I'll be sleeping with my new lover, Frank.

Although I might not get too much sleep, Pansy." She giggled behind a delicate finger.

"Hold on Gemma, you've forgotten something." Karlene held a small metal cage. "Pansy isn't allowed to cum. We don't want Lily playing with Pansy's little missy when they should be getting their beauty sleep."

Gemma giggled and took the device from Karlene. She clipped it onto Pansy's genitals before he could react. She clipped shut a small padlock. The cage linked around the base of his balls. His clitty was trapped almost flat in a tiny cage of around half an inch long.

"It's squashing my dick flat, Gemma, take it off."

Gemma smiled at him. "You know you don't have a dick, Pansy, don't be a silly sissy. Now stop complaining and put on your cute little nightie."

Karlene passed a pink baby-doll. Lily was already changed into a pink nightie and she hopped into the bed, waiting with the covers up for Pansy.

"Why is this cage so small?" Pansy complained.

Gemma undressed Pansy and pulled the baby doll nightie over his head. It finished above his cage. Karlene put her fingers to the little cage. "We're reducing the size further. By restricting the cage to half an inch, little missy will eventually shrivel in size. I think that's more appropriate for a little sissy boy like you."

"No. Don't do this." His eyes watered.

They ignored his protests. Gemma lifted the pink covers of the bed. "Come on, Pansy-puff, into bed like a good sissy. Cuddle up next to your sissy girlfriend, Lily."

Pansy climbed in with a show of reluctance. Lily snuggled in tight next to him. Gemma pulled the covers up to Pansy's face and kissed him on the forehead.

"Please can I come and sleep with you." He pouted

Karlene sat next to Gemma on the bed. "Be a good sissy-boy," she said lovingly. "I told you that Sir is sleeping with Goddess Gemma. Remember? You're a little pansy princess who couldn't satisfy me,

Goddess Gemma. You had your chance and failed. So now I have Sir to deal with that. Goodnight Pansy."

Gemma and Karlene got up together. "Be a good sissy, go straight to sleep. You've had a big day. You'll need your energy again for tomorrow. Lily needs lots of love and I need a good sissy maid."

Gemma turned to Frank and stroked his cock through his jeans. "Let's go, big boy. I need this one more time before we go to sleep. Or maybe twice." She looked up at Karlene and winked. "I can't get enough."

Pansy sat up. Karlene raised a finger to him and he laid down again. Gemma and Frank walked out to the hall outside the bedroom. They looked at each other again as Pansy looked on in fear. Gemma's hand brushed against the outline of the enormous cock again and she grinned mischievously at Pansy.

"Let's retire to our bedroom, big boy lover," Gemma said.

"Yes, I would like that," Frank boomed.

They left for the master bedroom, their feet patting on the hall carpet. Karlene left the room and closed the door to Pansy's room. Lily was already asleep. She put an ear to the door. She wanted to make sure Princess Pansy was being a good little girl before retiring to the guest bedroom at the front of the house.

The only sounds from inside were two soft snores.

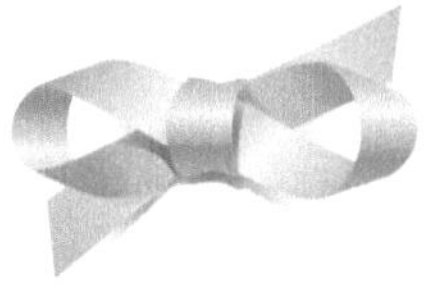

11 — Consequences

Karlene walked into the kitchen the next morning. It was early and the smell of fresh coffee and toast wafted in the air.

Gemma was sitting alone at a large pine country-style kitchen table, drinking from a white mug. Her eyes were smaller and more tired than usual. It had been a long night for her. Karlene had heard them at it until three in the morning from the guest room next door. Next time, she'd sleep downstairs on the sofa.

They greeted each other and Gemma poured a cup of coffee out for Karlene. Gemma told her Pansy had gone into the office to work, Frank had left for his Yoga studio and Lily had gone to her job at a female hairdressers where she was the assistant.

"I didn't like seeing Pansy in a male business suit," she told Karlene.

"We can discuss what to do about Pansy. She needs to continue running her business to pay for your luxuries; she has to keep you in the style you deserve. But, things need to change."

Gemma nodded. "What do you suggest, Karlene?"

Karlene leant forward as if she had a secret. "I've been thinking about this."

She laughed and Gemma smiled a knowing grin. "I guessed you would." Her eyes were watery and sleepy.

"We should send Pansy to work wearing pink lingerie under her suit."

"That would be fun," Gemma said with little enthusiasm.

Karlene spotted Gemma's lukewarm replies but pressed on. "And you could send sexy, detailed messages about all the fun you're having at home with your big, sexy boyfriend. Selfie photos of you sucking on his erection and so on." Karlene was pleased her plan had worked so well last night. "You got the hang of this very quickly, Gemma darling." She touched the back of Gemma's hand. "And I am always around to keep a loving eye out and to help you."

"I have Pansy's credit card." Gemma confided. "It's time to go online and buy a few things. I never spoiled myself before, I always felt guilty. Now I will. And of course, I'm going to buy presents for my stud of a boyfriend."

"The man of the house," Karlene replied, pleased to see Gemma perking up. She was probably tired. She would be fine after another caffeine kick.

Gemma opened up the white laptop sitting on the table. "I want to buy my sweet pansy princess lots more girly outfits. And you deserve gifts, Karlene, for everything you've shown me. None of this would have been possible were it not for you. And Pansy will pay for everything. She is wealthy. And she will love her new cuckold pansy lifestyle."

Karlene touched Gemma's hand again. Everything had gone according to her plan. She had been concerned Gemma's love for her husband would be too big an obstacle to overcome. Gemma had proved her concerns wrong and had realised she had to show her love through feminising and cuckolding her husband. It was what he desired. It was her sign of love for him.

Karlene knew it was time to push on with the next element of Pansy's transformation: diet, muscle loss and surgery. Karlene's mind turned to an image of Pansy with 38DD boobs. Perfect. She would need to tread carefully, Gemma still needed time to take in the transformation in her relationship with her husband.

Further down the line, Pansy's little clitty would have shrunk to half an inch and be useless after all that time locked up. Karlene sighed, she so hated how even a little clitty and pussy balls spoiled the front outline of a pretty sissy in a cute little skirt.

She stopped daydreaming. Back to now. "Now Pansy is dressed as a sissy, sleeping in a little princess's bedroom, we need to change sissy's diet and lifestyle."

Karlene observed Gemma, looking for any signs she was wavering. Gemma's face showed interest. But. Something wasn't right. Karlene couldn't put her finger on it.

"We need to put her on a new workout, none of this weight-lifting nonsense, that's for real men. Like Frank."

"I hadn't thought of that, Karlene, you have it all worked out."

Was that sarcasm? Karlene decided she was looking for something that wasn't there; she was feeling paranoid this morning. Hadn't everything gone perfectly last? Hadn't Gemma cuckolded her husband then pushed him into playing with Lily? Yes, there was nothing to worry about. Yet, she couldn't help feeling a nagging doubt about Gemma this morning.

"So what did you have in mind?" Gemma asked, taking a sip of her hot coffee.

Karlene decided to ignore her inner doubting voices and plough on. "Reduce her calorie and protein intake and feed her salad. Enrol her in an aerobics class with other girls, dressed in tight bottoms and a sports bra. Everything to get rid of her muscles and make her slimmer. We need to change her figure to something more appropriate for a sissy princess. Muscles don't suit an effeminate pansy boy."

"I see. I suppose you're right."

There it was again. Something isn't right. A distinct lack of enthusiasm.

"And you might need another boyfriend, maybe two or three?" Karlene changed the subject to her boyfriend. Gemma had been full of enthusiasm for that last night. At last, she had a real man and a big cock.

Gemma looked into her coffee.

12 — Eviction

Karlene left Gemma mulling over her breakfast. What was wrong with her? She had seemed to have been enjoying herself and there she was moping the next morning. Karlene had other concerns and returned to her apartment to deal with some urgent tax affairs. Just when she was enjoying the feeling of turning another man into a sissy princess, the Government steps in to ruin her mindset.

Paul Paige's sissification had been especially satisfying. Turning Paul Paige into a cuckold pansy with the help of his own wife. That had been special indeed and her plan to become a Mistress tutor had started well with Gemma. Karlene's head was full of plans, the things she could do to Pansy. The sky was the limit. 40DD boobs, why not? A massive Kardashian-like bottom? Absolutely. If only she'd have thought of all that when she knew him in college. He would have been a willing object of her plans.

Karlene sent her income documents and costs over to her accountant, thankful that was out of the way for now. She spent the rest of the day dealing with messages from clients and was interested in two from prospective females wanting to know more about her Mistress training programme.

She left her place in the early evening to head for Gemma and Pansy's home. She wanted to be there to see how things were and be there before Pansy got back from the office.

She arrived by taxi and Gemma greeted her warmly. She seemed to have recovered her from her unhappy mood earlier. Frank was already there, he had left his assistant in charge of gym classes for the evening. He wanted more hot sex with Gemma. Goodness, he was insatiable, maybe she should have kept hold of him and not passed him to Gemma. Never mind, needs must and there were plenty more where that came from; big dicks, big muscles, small brains.

Gemma showed Karlene to the living room and excused herself, saying she wanted to get ready for when Pansy got back. She wanted to keep the pressure on. This was good.

This left Karlene sitting in the living room with Frank. He was not one of the world's biggest conversationalists. He answered her questions with a yes, no or a grunt. He did have the most amazing muscles and a cock to die for. Karlene counted five times last night that he came. His powers of regeneration were amazing. Unable to get any kind of conversation going, she thought about telling him to get his cock out for her to play with for some light relief.

He was dressed in sportswear that evening. He wore a gym vest which was loose and low-fronted and accentuated his chest muscles. His arms were massive. He was in track trousers, his long cock clear and loose, flopping in a leg inside them.

"Say Frank, why don't you get your trouser snake out? I need some entertainment."

"Sure," Frank said, without much thought. He dug into his track trousers and whipped out his cock. He rubbed it with a wide grin on his face and, within seconds, it stood up long and hard.

Karlene was about to get up and sit next to him to play with it when she heard Gemma stomping around upstairs. What was she up to? Her eyes fell on Frank as he played with himself. His face was blank. "Don't cum, Frank, there's a good boy. We don't want a mess on Gemma's nice carpet. Keep it hard for me though."

"Yes, Mistress Karlene." Daniel rubbed more gently, looking like a scolded schoolboy.

The sound of footsteps coming down the stairs alerted Karlene to Gemma's arrival. She imagined her looking sexy in a short sexy dress with her boobs spilling out. Karlene wore a tiny tight skirt, super high heels and a bra-like top which only just kept her breasts in. Time for a repeat of last night. What fun.

Gemma slunk into the room. She was dressed casually, a loose top that hid her large firm breasts. She wore blue slacks and flat shoes. Her eyes went to Frank who beamed at her as he rubbed his cock. She scowled. "Put it away, stupid."

"I thought you were getting ready, Gemma dear," said Karlene now perturbed at her turn of mood again.

Before she could answer they heard the front door open. Karlene got up, Frank continued to rub his erection as he was so carried away, her instruction to put it away didn't sink in.

"In here, Pansy," Karlene called. Sir's got a gift waiting for you."

Gemma gave a watery smile. Karlene decided to push on, Gemma was probably still tired from last night's exertions.

Pansy entered the living room, sheepishly. He wore a dark-blue business suit and tan shoes. His dark hair was swept back again and over the collar of a stiff blue cotton shirt. If Karlene hadn't seen Paul in action as a sissy femboy last night, she would have thought him the successful powerful businessman again. She knew under the expensive suit, lay a sissy princess and she wanted him this way from now on. Before he fell back into manhood.

Pansy saw Frank playing with his enormous erection: his expression dropped in despair. He'd obviously hoped Frank was a one-off.

Karlene stood and stepped forward. Gemma wasn't doing anything. What was wrong with her? She would need to take action to pull her out of her mood. She unbuttoned Pansy's suit jacket and threw it over the sofa. She undid his tie and slid it around inside his collar and discarded it on top of the jacket. Once she had Pansy back in his little pansy clothes again, this tense situation with Gemma would resolve and it would be like last night.

She should tell Frank to work on Gemma while Pansy watched again and sobbed. Maybe Frank could take Gemma from behind while she squealed in sexual joy and ecstasy at having his eleven inches of pure testosterone inside her. That would perk her up. All the while, Pansy would have to watch, sobbing with his little miss clitty held in by a tiny cock cage.

Soon he would no longer be Paul Paige, but once again the little pansy femboy he always was inside. She popped the first button of his shirt open, then the second button, then the third. She ripped it open to his belly as he looked down. He offered no resistance. Good, they had broken his resistance last night.

An arm came between them."Enough."

Karlene looked askance. Gemma stood glaring, her face fixed in determination.

"What are you doing, Gemma?" asked Karlene.

"I'm stopping this."

Karlene didn't understand, her face was fixed in disbelief. What was wrong with Gemma? Last night she'd been full of wonder at the unfolding events. Gemma grabbed Karlene by her forearm and marched her out of the living room. She pulled her to the front door, opened it and shoved her out. They faced each other. Karlene in shock, Gemma in stern assurance.

"It's finished. I don't know what came over me. I must have been crazy to have listened to you. I was hypnotised. It was a kind of madness. My goodness, what have I done to my husband?"

Karlene stared from the front step in shock. "But, it was what he wanted. You were giving him his dream, darling."

"Don't darling me, Karlene. Go away and never come back. I don't want to see you ever again. Go. Now." Gemma pointed out into the distance.

She slammed the door, the walls shook, a vase fell from a small wooden table and shattered on the floor. Gemma hardly noticed.

She marched back into the living room. Paul stood in surprise, his shirt open to his belly, his face bathed in shock. Frank sat on the other side of the room by the sofa. His hand was still around his cock, but not moving. Gemma strode up to Frank. She swung her foot and connected with his hanging balls. He doubled up, fighting for breath. She swung a fist to his nose and it squashed hard. A trickle of blood ran from one nostril. He touched his nose, his face blank and uncomprehending. He looked up. "Uh?"

"GET OUT OF MY HOUSE YOU HORRIBLE MAN," Gemma screamed.

Despite being a foot taller than Gemma, he complied and got up and hobbled to the door, trying to pull up his track bottoms, tripping as he went. Gemma's foot connected with his bottom and he hurried. Gemma followed, passed him and opened the front door. Frank fell out, tripped and fell face-first on the concrete footpath next to Karlene, still standing in disbelief. Gemma slammed the door.

She rushed back to her husband. She threw herself at him, kissing his face all over. He was in a confused trance. Gemma pulled him to the sofa, her hands at his trouser flies, she pulled off his trousers, removed his underpants and laid him along the sofa. She went down to his little penis, it was soft. She put her mouth over it and gobbled at it ravenously. It grew to its full three inches. She pulled her own trousers off in a rush, removed her panties and settled back down on top of him. She twisted her hips, took his erection with one hand and placed it inside her. She couldn't feel it but she didn't care.

"I love you so much. Please forgive me. Please. I was so stupid to involve other people in our life."

They moved together. His hard little penis was perfect inside her. It wasn't about size or the fact she couldn't feel it, it was about them.

"Please tell me you forgive me. I want to be with you. I want to forget about Karlene and Frank. Tell me you'll forgive me."

They ground their bodies together more rapidly and Paul came. She could tell only by his gasps. Gemma flopped on top of him once he stopped. She'd use her battery-operated dildo later. Their breathing slowed.

"Gemma?" said Paul from beside her.

Gemma looked up into his eyes.

"I love you more than anything, Gemma my love. I'm devoted to you. I'm loyal to you. It's the only reason I went along with all that stupidity last night. Let's forget it and pick up as if nothing else ever happened. Everyone can make a mistake. You were entranced by Karlene and that hunk of meat with the huge cock but at least you came to your senses before it got even more out of hand."

Gemma hugged him tight, tears of joy fell down her cheeks and onto her husband's chest. Her cheek lay on his chest and she felt his heart beating. Gemma hugged him harder and her head sunk further into him. "Thank you, thank you. I'm so sorry."

Paul stroked her hair. "So we'll forget everything that happened?"

Gemma raised her head and looked at him. Her smile was weak but genuine. The smile died away. "Not everything." She smiled again and she stroked his hair with a gentle touch.

"There are going to be a few changes in our marriage."

He pushed himself up on one elbow and his face creased with concern.

She smiled with a sparkle in her eyes. "A lot of changes indeed. Pansy Princess."

. . ❧ . .

END OF SISSY HUSBAND 2

. . ❧ . .

I hope you enjoyed this novel. If so, please leave me a review on the site where you bought it.
Thank you

Lady Alexa

Don't miss out!

Visit the website below and you can sign up to receive emails whenever Lady Alexa publishes a new book. There's no charge and no obligation.

https://books2read.com/r/B-A-JTBM-TMJLF

BOOKS 2 READ

Connecting independent readers to independent writers.

Did you love *Sissy Husband 2*? Then you should read *SIssy Husband 1*[1] by Lady Alexa!

[2]

Paul Paige has a deep secret from his wife, Gemma. He is a secret sissy femboy who visits professional ladies for a few hours of feminisation.However, he contacts Mistress Karlene who knows him and his sissy desires from when they dated ten years previously. Karlene befriends Gemma and tells her about her husband's femboy side. After first being annoyed, Karlene shows Gemma the benefits of having a femboy husband, not least because of his failures in bed. Paul's future suddenly looks very different.

This novel contains explicit scenes of a sexual nature including forced male to female gender transformation, female domination, humiliation, cuckolding, spanking and feminisation. All characters in this story are

---

1. https://books2read.com/u/49A5gp

2. https://books2read.com/u/49A5gp

aged 18 and over. Strictly for adults aged 18 and over or the age of maturity in your country.

Read more at https://www.ladyalexauk.com.

Also by Lady Alexa

Becoming Joanne
Becoming Joanne 1
Becoming Joanne 2
Becoming Joanne 3

Femboy Love
Femboy Love 1

Feminized and Pretty
Feminized and Pretty 1
Feminized and Pretty 3
Feminized and Pretty 4

Forced Feminization
Forced Feminization Bundle 1

Lockdown Feminization

Lockdown Feminization 3
Lockdown Feminization 1

Sissy femboy transgender husband
Sissy Husband 2
Sissy Husband 3
SIssy Husband 1
Sissy Husband 4

Sissy Princess
Sissy Princess 2
Sissy Princess 1

Stepmother's Sissy
Stepmother's Sissy
Stepmother's Sissy 2
Stepmother's Sissy 3

Standalone
A Very Dominant Woman
Sissy Pink

Watch for more at https://www.ladyalexauk.com.

About the Author

I am an author and blogger on female led relationships, encouraged feminization and femdom and other erotica.

Read more at https://www.ladyalexauk.com.